THIS

SWEET PICKLES ®

BOOK
BELONGS TO

_____

In the world of *Sweet Pickles,* each animal
gets into a pickle because of an all too human
personality trait.

This book is about X-rating Xerus, who thinks
that telling people what is not allowed
will solve all problems.

Books in the Sweet Pickles Series

WHO STOLE ALLIGATOR'S SHOE?
SCAREDY BEAR
FIXED BY CAMEL
NO KICKS FOR DOG
ELEPHANT EATS THE PROFITS
FISH AND FLIPS
GOOSE GOOFS OFF
HIPPO JOGS FOR HEALTH
ME TOO IGUANA
JACKAL WANTS MORE
WHO CAN TRUST YOU, KANGAROO?
LION IS DOWN IN THE DUMPS
MOODY MOOSE BUTTONS

NUTS TO NIGHTINGALE
OCTOPUS PROTESTS
PIG THINKS PINK
QUAIL CAN'T DECIDE
REST RABBIT REST
STORK SPILLS THE BEANS
TURTLE THROWS A TANTRUM
HAPPY BIRTHDAY UNICORN
KISS ME, I'M VULTURE
VERY WORRIED WALRUS
XERUS WON'T ALLOW IT
YAKETY YAK YAK YAK
ZIP GOES ZEBRA

Library of Congress Cataloging in Publication Data

Hefter, Richard.
  Xerus won't allow it.

  (Sweet Pickles series)
  SUMMARY: Xerus is convinced that more rules and
regulations will keep order in the town of Sweet
Pickles, until she finds that she has to follow the
rules too.
  [1. Squirrels—Fiction] I. Title. II. Series.
PZ7.H3587Xe   [E]   77-16321
ISBN 0-03-042076-8

Weekly Reader Books presents

XERUS
WON'T
ALLOW IT

Written and Illustrated
by Richard Hefter
Edited by Ruth Lerner Perle

Holt, Rinehart and Winston · New York

Xerus was standing in front of the bank talking to Rabbit when Yak pulled up in his cab.

"Hey, Yak!" yelled Rabbit. "You can't park there, you are blocking traffic!"

"I have to make a deposit," said Yak, "and there is no law against parking here. And besides, I have a lot to do today and I am in a hurry so I don't have time to talk right now because I am very busy. You told me yourself that it was important to stay on schedule and I always listen to what people tell me. And furthermore..."

"But, Yak," wailed Rabbit, "you can't park here."

"That's right!" said Xerus.

Traffic was backed up all along Main Street.
Horns were honking. Everyone was getting angry.
"There's only one way to stop this!" announced Xerus.
She ran home and got out her paint and a board and
made a sign.

When Xerus got back to the bank, Rabbit and Yak were still yelling. Horns were honking. Traffic was all blocked up and things were even worse than before.

"Please," cried Rabbit, "move your car, Yak. Everyone is stuck and no one can get past you."

"That's the trouble around here," said Yak. "Everyone is always in a hurry. No one has time to sit down and talk. Why, just the other day…"

"Read this!" screeched Xerus. She put her sign down right in front of Yak.

The sign said: NO PARKING IN FRONT OF BANK. NO STOPPING. NO STANDING. NO TALKING.

"Well, why didn't someone tell me it was against the law?" mumbled Yak. "I always obey the law. Ask anyone if I don't. Why, just yesterday I was saying to…"

Yak started his cab and drove off.

Traffic started to move again on Main Street.

"Thank you, Xerus," said Rabbit. "That sign is just what we need around here."

Xerus smiled.

"The real trouble around here," she said, "is that there aren't enough signs and no one knows what is not allowed!"

She walked into the park.
Alligator and Elephant were eating sandwiches. Jackal and Nightingale were playing ball. Goose was sleeping under a tree.

Suddenly, Nightingale threw the ball. The ball bounced off Elephant's trunk. It bounced into Alligator's sandwiches and landed on Goose's head.

"Oh dear," smiled Elephant, "that was a close one."
"Close!" screamed Alligator. "That ball landed right in
my food and probably spoiled it, and it's all
Nightingale's fault!"

"Nyaah," screeched Nightingale. "Serves you right!
You ought to watch where you're eating."
"You little runt!" yelled Alligator. "I'll get you
for that."

Alligator started to chase Nightingale around the tree.

Goose opened one eye. "What's going on around here?" she yawned. "Can't a person sleep in peace?"

"This crazy Alligator is after me," shouted Nightingale.

"That nasty Nightingale spoiled my food," yelled Alligator.

"Now, now, you two," said Elephant, "stop it."

"Nuts to you!" screamed Nightingale.

Pretty soon everyone was running around the tree and shouting.

"I can stop this," said Xerus, and she went home and painted another sign.

When she got back to the park, Alligator and
Nightingale and Goose and Elephant and Jackal were
still arguing.

Xerus marched up to them and stuck her sign in the
ground.

It said: NO BALL PLAYING IN PICNIC AREA.
           NO EATING ON BALL FIELD.
           NO SLEEPING. NO YELLING.

The argument stopped.
Elephant and Alligator stopped eating.
Nightingale and Jackal stopped playing ball.
Goose went home. "I need to rest," she yawned.
"Whoever heard of a park you can't sleep in?"

"I knew it," grinned Xerus. "What this town really needs is more rules and regulations. Then everyone will know what not to do."

Xerus was on her way home when she passed the candy store. Vulture was going in. Moose was coming out. They collided in the doorway with a loud BUMP.

"Why don't you look where you're going?" grumbled Moose.

"Why don't you?" mumbled Vulture.

"I was here first," said Moose with a frown.

"But I was going in," said Vulture, "and that's more important. Now move aside."

"I won't!" shouted Moose.

"You will!" screamed Vulture.

"I can straighten this out," cackled Xerus, and she ran home to make another sign.

When she got back to the candy store, Vulture and
Moose were still in the doorway. They were still arguing.
Xerus put up her sign. It said:
          ABSOLUTELY NO GOING IN THE OUT.
          POSITIVELY NO GOING OUT THE IN.
          NO IN OR OUT ALLOWED.
Moose read the sign. Vulture read the sign. They looked
at each other. They looked at the sign again.
They both stepped out of the doorway and went home.

"Well," said Xerus, "I solved another problem."

"But now no one can go into the candy store," moaned Elephant.

"Or come out of it either," cried Walrus from inside the store.

"Rules are rules," shouted Xerus. She ran home to make more signs.

Xerus stayed up all night painting signs.
"Rules and regulations are what this town needs," she
screeched.

In the morning, Xerus rushed out and put her signs up all over town.

Elephant couldn't find any place to eat.

Yak couldn't park his taxi. And he couldn't talk to anyone about it.

Quail couldn't stay on the grass. Quail couldn't get off the grass.

All over Sweet Pickles everything ground to a halt.

"Help!" cried Walrus from the candy store.

"Help!" cried Elephant. "I'm hungry!"

"Help, help, help," whispered Yak.

"Did I hear a call for help?" laughed Zebra, as he zipped by pulling his wagon. "I could use some help myself... I've spent the whole morning taking down these silly signs."

"Silly signs! Of course!" exclaimed Elephant. She pulled up a NO EATING sign and took out a sandwich.

Octopus pulled up a NO SITTING sign. Quail sat down.

Everybody pitched in. They took down all the signs.

"Phew!" sighed Walrus, as he came out of the candy store. "That was getting to be a problem."

"It's not over yet," laughed Zebra. "There's one more sign to take care of. Come on."

Everybody followed Zebra.

Xerus was in her house painting more signs when she heard a knock on the door.

She opened the door.

There, in front of her, was the biggest sign she had ever seen. It said:

SIGN PAINTING
ABSOLUTELY
NOT ALLOWED!

"Well!" sighed Xerus. "Rules are rules."

She put down her paintbrush and stopped painting signs.

"I'm glad there's no rule about stickers," she said.
Xerus got out a crayon and lots of little stickers.
She started writing...
No parking in front of bank. No ball playing in the park.
No sleeping. No standing. No walking. No running.
No jumping. Do not litter. No loitering...

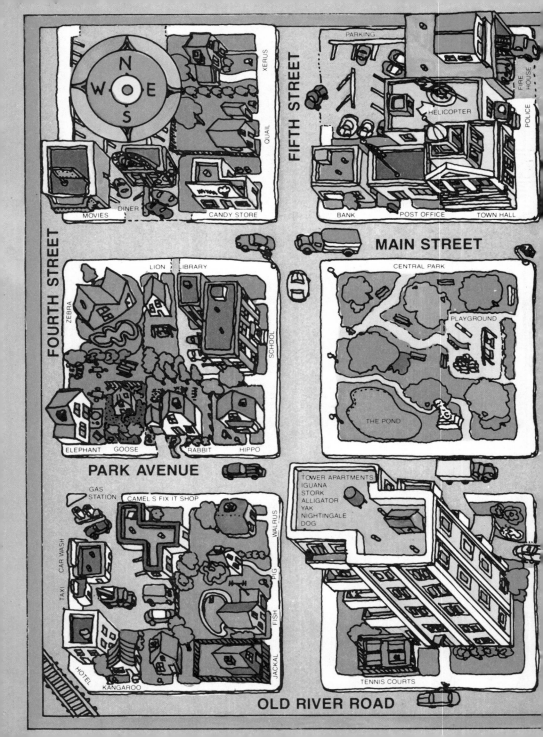